Dear Parents,

Congratulations! Your child has embarked on an exciting journey – they're learning to read! As a parent, you can be there to support and cheer them along as they take their first steps.

At school, children are taught how to decode words and arrange these building blocks of language into sentences and wonderful stories.

At home, parents play a vital part in reinforcing these new-found skills. You can help your child practise their reading by providing well-written, engaging stories, which you can enjoy together.

This series – **Ready, Steady, Read!** – offers exactly that, and more. These stories support inexperienced readers by:

- gradually introducing new vocabulary
- using repetition to consolidate learning
- gradually increasing sentence length and word count
- providing texts that boost a young reader's confidence.

As each book is completed, engaging activities encourage young readers to look back at the story, while a Picture Dictionary reinforces new vocabulary. Enjoyment is the key – and reading together can be great fun for both parent and child!

Prue Goodwin
Lecturer in Literacy and Children's Books

The **Ready, Steady, Read!** series has 4 levels.
The facing page shows what you can expect to find
in the books at each level.

As your child's confidence grows, they can progress
to books from the higher levels. These will keep them
engaged and encourage new reading skills.

The levels are only meant as guides; together, you and
your child can pick the book that will be just right.

Here are some handy tips for helping children who are
ready for reading!

 Give them choice – Letting children pick a book
(from the level that's right for them) makes them
feel involved.

Talk about it – Discussing the story and the
pictures helps children engage with the book.

Read it again – Repetition of favourite stories
reinforces learning.

Cheer them on! – Praise and encouragement
builds a child's confidence and the belief in their
growing ability.

LEVEL 1 For first readers

* short, straightforward sentences
* basic, fun vocabulary
* simple, easy-to-follow stories of up to 100 words
* large print and easy-to-read design

LEVEL 2 For developing readers

* longer sentences
* simple vocabulary, introducing new words
* longer stories of up to 200 words
* bold design, to capture readers' interest

LEVEL 3 For more confident readers

* longer sentences with varied structure
* wider vocabulary
* high-interest stories of up to 300 words
* smaller print for experienced readers

LEVEL 4 For able readers

* longer sentences with complex structure
* rich, exciting vocabulary
* complex stories of up to 400 words
* emphasis on text more than illustrations

Once you have read the story, you will find some amazing activities at the back of the book! There are Excellent Exercises for you to complete, plus a super Picture Dictionary.

But first it is time for the story . . .

Ready?
Steady?
Let's read!

A H Benjamin   Gwyneth Williamson

Little Mouse
and the Big, Red Apple

LITTLE TIGER PRESS
London

Mouse was feeling hungry one day,
when he came across a big, red apple.
"I will take it home and have a
feast!" he cried.

Mouse rolled the apple
over and over.

"Yum, yum," he thought.
Suddenly . . .

SPLASH!

. . . the apple rolled into a pond.

"Oh no!" wailed Mouse.

"Don't worry," said Frog. "I will help you."

Frog kicked the apple with his strong legs.

It flew out of the water.

BUMP!

Frog licked his lips.

"Thanks," said Mouse as he went
on his way. He did not want to share
his apple with Frog.

Just then . . .

the apple
fell into a
thorn bush.

"Ouch!" cried
Mouse, as he
tried to rescue
his dinner.
"These prickles
hurt."

"I will help you," said Tortoise.
"My shell will protect me."

Tortoise brought Mouse the apple
and stroked it, longingly.

"Thanks," said Mouse as he went on his way. He did not want to share his apple with Tortoise.

Suddenly . . .

. . . the apple rolled into a log.

"Oh no!" cried Mouse.

"I will help you," said Mole. And she
dug a tunnel right under the log.

It was just wide enough for the apple
to go through.

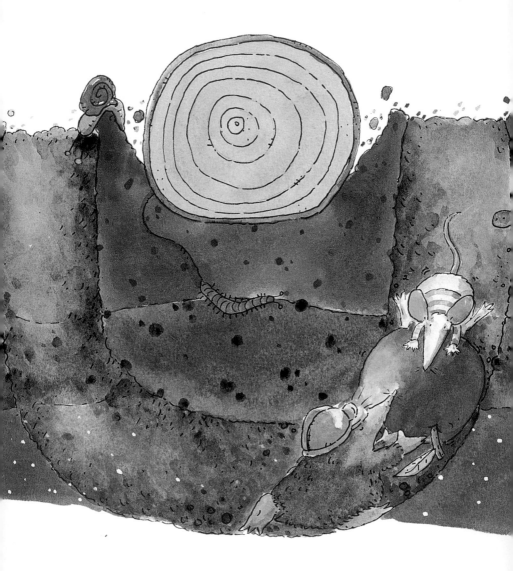

Mole sniffed the apple.

"Thanks," said Mouse as he went
on his way. He did not want to share
his apple with Mole.

Mouse came
to a steep hill.

Up, up, up
went Mouse . . .

to the very top. "Home at last,"
he sighed, happily.
But then Mouse
let go . . .

. . . and the apple rolled
back down the hill.

Faster . . .

and faster until . . .

. . . it hit the bottom.

Mouse ran down . . .

But when he got there . . .

. . . Frog, Mole and Tortoise were already chomping!

"How kind of you to send us the apple," cried Mole.

Mouse gave a big sigh.

"That's what friends are for," he said.

Excellent Exercises

Have you read the story? Well done!
Now it is time for more fun!

Here are some questions about the story. Ask an adult to
listen to your answers, and help if you get stuck.

Tasty Treat

In this story, Mouse does not want to share his big, red
apple. Is there anything that *you* find difficult to share?

Amazing Animals

Can you name all the animals in this picture?
What animals have *you* seen in the countryside?

Mouse and Mole

Now describe what is happening in this picture.

Hilltop Home

At the end of the story, Mouse pushes the apple to the very top of the hill. Can you remember what happens next?

Picture Dictionary

Can you read all of these words from the story?

apple

bush
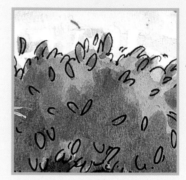

chomping

frog

legs

mole

mouse

push

red

tortoise

Can you think of any other words that describe these pictures – for example, what colours can you see? Why not try to spell some of these words? Ask an adult to help!

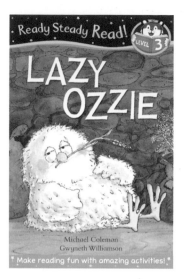

Lazy Ozzie

Lazy Ozzie is too lazy to learn how to fly. So he thinks of a brilliant plan to fool his mum into thinking he can. But will Ozzie's mum be so easily fooled . . . ?

Nobody Laughs at a Lion!

"I'm the King of the Jungle because I'm the best!" says Pa Lion. But each time he shows off his skills, the other animals start to giggle. Don't they know that NOBODY laughs at a lion?

Ridiculous!

One snowy day, Shelley
leaves her cosy bed
to go on an adventure.
But whoever heard of a
tortoise out in winter . . . ?
Ridiculous!

Who's Been Eating My Porridge?

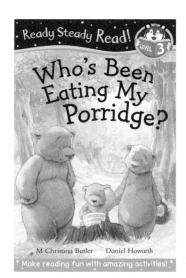

Little Bear will not eat his
porridge. So his mother
gives it to Old Scary Bear
in the woods. Little Bear
does not believe in the
Scary Bear. But *someone*
has been eating his
porridge . . . !

For Dave — A H B
For Jamie and Joseph — G W

LITTLE TIGER PRESS, 1 The Coda Centre, 189 Munster Road, London SW6 6AW
First published in Great Britain 2000
This edition published 2013
Text copyright © A H Benjamin 2000, 2013
Illustrations copyright © Gwyneth Williamson 2000, 2013
All rights reserved
Printed in China
978-1-84895-674-2
LTP/1800/0594/0413
2 4 6 8 10 9 7 5 3 1

Books in the Series

LEVEL 1 – For first readers

Can't You Sleep, Dotty?

Fred

My Turn!

Rosie's Special Surprise

What Bear Likes Best!

LEVEL 2 – For developing readers

Hopping Mad!

Newton

Ouch!

Where There's a Bear, There's Trouble!

The Wish Cat

LEVEL 3 – For more confident readers

Lazy Ozzie

Little Mouse and the Big Red Apple

Nobody Laughs at a Lion!

Ridiculous!

Who's Been Eating My Porridge?

LEVEL 4 – For able readers

The Biggest Baddest Wolf

Meggie Moon

Mouse, Mole and the Falling Star

The Nutty Nut Chase

Robot Dog